For Mares and Henscott and Tom Rox
Tudor Humphries

First American edition published in 2009
by Boxer Books Limited.

Distributed in the United States and Canada by Sterling Publishing Co., Inc.
387 Park Avenue South, New York, NY 10016-8810

First published in Great Britain in 2009 by Boxer Books Limited.
www.boxerbooks.com

The illustrations were prepared using homemade watercolor paints.
The text is set in Adobe Caslon.

ISBN 978-1-906250-69-0

1 3 5 7 9 10 8 6 4 2

Printed in China

All of our papers are sourced from managed forests and renewable resources.

OTTER MOON

TUDOR HUMPHRIES

BOXER BOOKS

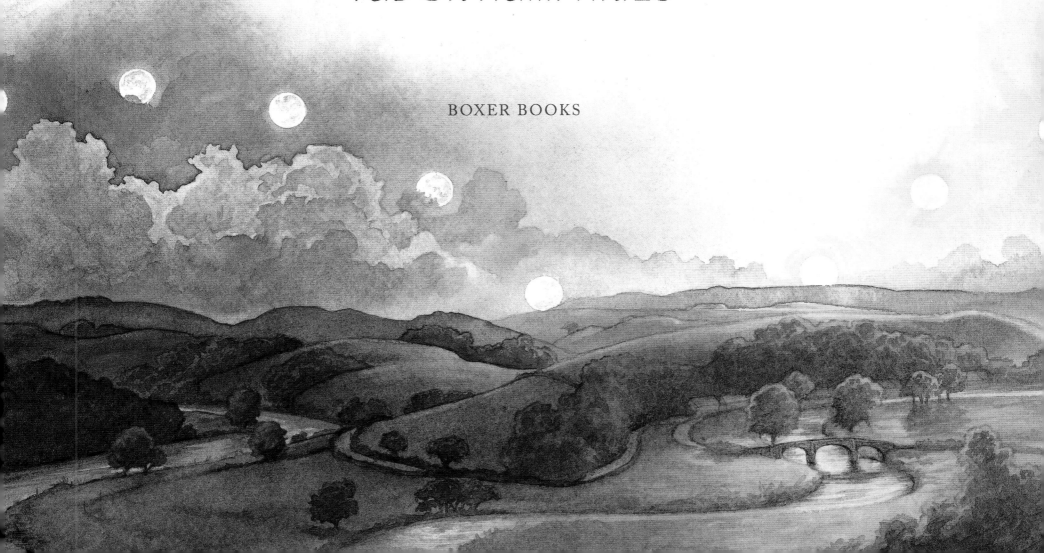

In the land of the otters, while we all slept,
Flibbertigibbet lay in his secret place, watching
the freckly moon rise over the wood.

Night was Day for him, and Day was Night.
A kingfisher flashed past, blue as a jewel,
going home, late for bed.

Flibberty loved the moon. He watched its face in the water, sparkling as the river ran over the stones.

"You're in trouble," the river seemed to burble, and he knew he probably was. He'd been sent to catch fish, but he had been chasing froglets and newts instead.

He watched the bats flying low over the water, swallowing moths.

Suddenly the King of the River came surging downstream and knocked him off his perch, bellowing, "Flibbertigibbet, why are you so lazy? Where is that fish I want on my dish?"

Flibberty flibbered and gibbered and floundered in the water in fright. The old King growled at him.

"Catch me a fish, and it had better be on a silver dish.
I want my dinner by first light!"

Flibberty slunk low into the water, feeling it fill his fur
and rise over his head. He swam off miserably downstream
like a wet cat, bumping into rocks and tangling in weed beds.
How could he catch a great fish before daybreak?
Where would he find a silver dish?

He rose for breath just as great pale wings swept over him, and the Heron stood on the riverbank, dressed in his suit of gray.

"I can help you," croaked the Heron. "Follow the river far downstream. Use your eyes; use your wits; find the dish. Before you know it, you'll find the fish."

All rivers run to the sea, and this one was no different,
so Flibberty followed the river. After a while, tired from
swimming, he stopped to look at the moon,
but the Heron urged him on.

"Flibberty, keep your mind on the fish!
There! I saw a glimmering gleam. . . ."

Flibberty thought he saw it too: a silver fish—
or was it a dish?—far away, glowing in the shadows and dark.
Instantly he was a hunter, alert and sharp. He chased it,
and the water whooshed him along.

But when he got there, there was no sign. The dish, or the fish, was gone. Hopeless again, Flibberty swam under the bridge and started downriver once more. After many hours of searching, he paused in the moonlight under a great tree, tired and hungry.

The Heron's watchful eye flickered over the shallows. He jabbed, and a slippery, slimy eel was in his beak. He shared it with the young otter and they set off again.

Then suddenly they thought they saw it. There, in the distance, they saw a glimmer of shimmering silver. Flibberty swam as fast as a flood and the Heron flew above.

But there was no fish, and certainly no silver dish—just the splish and splash of the river, hurrying to the sea.

All night Flibberty searched, and by first light he was in unknown country, farther than he'd ever swum before. The river had grown wider overnight as it drew nearer to the sea. Soon it would be daybreak, and he would have to tell the King that he hadn't found the fish or the silver dish. He felt lonely and afraid, and he wanted the Heron to feel sorry for him. But the Heron was nowhere to be seen.

Flibberty was all alone under the fading stars, and the sky was growing bright.

He rounded a bend, and there was the King of the River, scowling from his throne, hungry and angry, brewing like a storm. Flibberty climbed slowly out of the water and up the bank, trembling and stumbling over roots and rocks, to tell the King that he had failed.

But the old King Otter rose and stood stock-still. Then he raised his great paw and pointed over Flibbertigibbet's shoulder. "I can see the silver dish! You've left it in the water. But where is the fish?"

Flibberty didn't know how to answer, or how a shining silver dish could have appeared behind him, but at that moment, as he turned . . .

a great fish . . .

dropped from the sky
and landed . . .

slap . . .

on the shimmering dish.

The King was astonished. They gazed at the fish
on the dish for a long, long time before they ate
it and fell soundly asleep.

Then Night became Day, and for them—the King
and Flibbertigibbet—Day became Night.

And the great silver dish that Flibberty had searched for,
for so long, turned slowly to gold.